# BAD FOOD

## Night of the Living Bread

By Eric Luper

Illustrated by
"The Doodle Boy" Joe Whale

Scholastic Inc.

# SCHOOL MAP

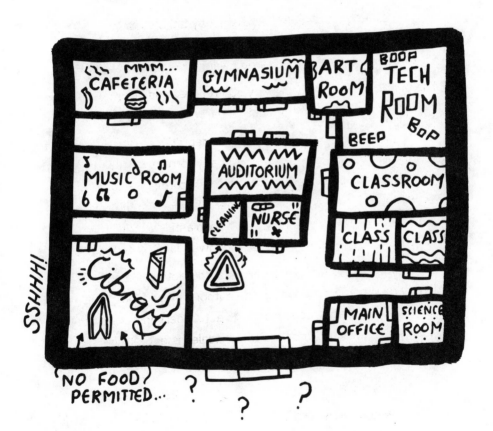

# CHAPTER 1

## Around the "Glampfire"

**N**ight had come to Belching Walrus Elementary. The doors were locked, the hallways were empty, and the lights in the Cafeteria were dimmed. The only light came from one single burner on one single stove. Food from the Pantry, the Cooler, and the Freezer huddled around the light to hear Glizzy, the oldest hot dog in the Cafeteria, tell his spooky stories. The blue flame from the burner reflected off his

tinfoil wrapping, making long, creepy shadows on the walls and lighting the faces of all the frightened, young food.

"...and when that donut got too close to the edge, she fell between the Freezer and the wall, never to be seen again," Glizzy whispered.

Pickles shrieked.

Onions cried.

Pretzels twisted.

Meanwhile, besties for all time Slice (a brave and cheesy slice of pizza), Scoop (a triple scoop ice cream cone—vanilla, chocolate, AND strawberry), and Totz (a crunchy, delicious, and trendy tater tot) stood nearby.

"I'm so excited for our camping trip," Slice said.

"Yeah," Totz said, tuning his banjo. "We've been so busy going on adventures that we haven't had time to relax."

"I'm not camping," Scoop said.

"You're not?" Slice and Totz said.

"Nope, I'm *glamping*," Scoop said. "It's camping but more glamorous."

"Hours turned to days," Glizzy said to the young food around the campfire. "Days turned to weeks. Soon, everyone in the Pantry began to hear moaning from behind the Freezer..."

GLAMOROUS + CAMPING= GLAMPING

A baby carrot gasped.

A fish stick cried for his mommy.

A Popsicle wet her wrapper a little.

"I don't believe Glizzy's stories for a second," Scoop said, safely away from the blue flame so she would not melt. "He just tells them to scare everyone."

"But it works," Slice said, his voice trembling. "I'm never going near the Freezer again."

"He's telling cautionary tales," Totz said.

"What's a cautionary tale?" Slice asked.

Totz leaned against the wall. "A cautionary tale is a story someone tells to warn of a danger. It's dangerous behind the Freezer, so the story warns us not to go there."

"I'd *melt* behind the Freezer," Scoop said. "I've heard it's hot."

"I'd probably go stale," Slice said. "Or the rats would eat me. Mus Musculus and his army nearly ate us all!"

"Ahem . . ."

Slice, Scoop, and Totz spun around. Glizzy and the rest of the campers were staring at them.

"I am the one telling the stories," Glizzy said. "Your whispering and your banjo playing are ruining the mood."

Scoop's strawberry ice cream turned brighter pink. "We're sorry," she said. "Please finish your story."

Glizzy turned back to the group. "One night, a night just like this one, a group of campers huddled around a campfire just like this one. They began to hear a strange noise. *Stomp-sliiide . . . Stomp-sliiide . . . Stomp-sliiide . . .*"

"What was it?" Cup of Yogurt asked.

Glizzy turned to Cup of Yogurt. "It was something different—something not quite alive but not quite *not* alive. The heat of the Freezer motor, the dust from the floor, and the spiders—oh, the spiders! That donut turned into something different," he said. "Some nights you can hear them walking around the Cafeteria. *Stomp-sliiide . . . Stomp-sliiide . . . Stomp-sliiide . . .* Some nights you can see shadows moving in the darkness. And some

nights . . ." Glizzy paused. "Some nights they come for you!"

Everyone, even Scoop, screamed.

"I want to go back to my fruit basket!" Banana cried.

"There is no need to worry," Sprinkles said, taking off her tattered zombie costume and wiping the green frosting from her face. "Just please stay away from the back of the Freezer. Now, let's look out the windows at some stars."

Scoop chuckled.

Slice shivered.

Totz said, "And that's Glizzy's cautionary tale."

As soon as they were in their sleeping bags, Glizzy started pointing out different constellations in the sky. "That's the Big Spatula," he said.

"And over there, just above that bright star, is Toaster Minor."

"And through that window," Sprinkles added, "is the scariest constellation of them all. It's called Tongue and Teeth."

"What's Tongue and Teeth?" a small cracker asked.

"No one knows for sure," Glizzy said. "But folks say it's the last thing food sees before they meet their end."

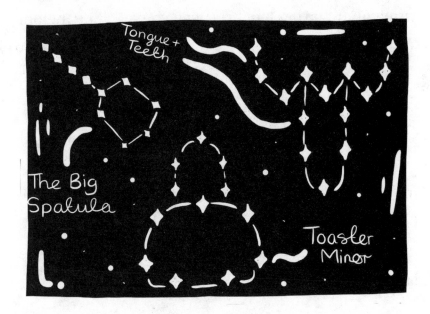

Scoop chuckled again. Slice shivered again.

"So, how are your painting lessons going?" Slice asked Totz.

"Great," he said. "Scoop is an amazing teacher. I've learned so much about colors, paint, and brush-strokes. Today, she taught me about 'blocking in.'"

"What's blocking in?" Slice asked.

"It's when you sketch your painting with pencil right on the canvas," Totz explained. "It helps make sure your painting looks the way you want it to before you start."

"Your family portrait is coming out so well," Scoop said.

"It's a big painting," Totz said. "I have a lot of brothers and sisters and aunts and uncles and cousins."

"You could be neater, though," Scoop said. "You're a bit messy with the paint."

Just as everyone was starting to doze off, the

Cafeteria doors flung open and the overhead lights went on one by one.

"What is the meaning of this?" Glizzy called down from the top of the stove.

"I might ask you the same thing," said Spex, a pair of glasses and the High Wizard of the Library. She marched in alongside Richard the dictionary and several stampers. "Food is not permitted in the Library."

"We know," Glizzy said. "That is why food does not *go* to the Library."

Spex stepped forward. "Then how do you explain this?"

She raised her hands. They were covered in red. "Ketchup!"

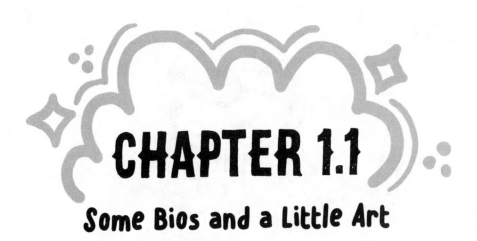

# CHAPTER 1.1

## Some Bios and a Little Art

In keeping with tradition, we should spend a moment reviewing a few character bios. It's always nice to refresh your memory between books, isn't it? Some of these characters may be important later in the story so don't skip this part and please pay close attention:

# Fry

Food Type: Donut (White Frosted)

Flavor: Sweeeeet!

Personality: Good sense of humor, friendly

Strengths: Deep knowledge of
food anatomy, good with tape

Weaknesses: Easily excited

Occupation: None (yet!)

Whereabouts: Currently at
the Nurse's Office attend-
ing medical school

# Mus Musculus

Food Type: Don't you dare eat a mouse!

Personality: A little unhinged

Strengths: Desire for world domination

Weaknesses: A little food obsessed

Hobbies: Tyrannical leader

Whereabouts: Unknown, likely doing the backstroke in the dumpster

Usually, we have a third character bio here, but instead we thought it would be fun to have a sneak peek at the family portrait Totz is working on . . .

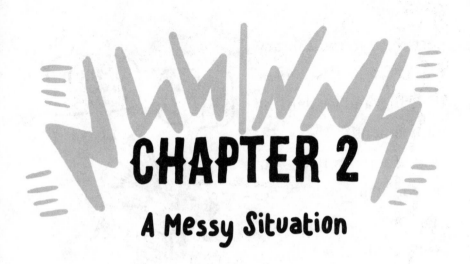

# CHAPTER 2

## A Messy Situation

**K**etchup?!" **everyone said** at once.

"Ketchup," Spex said. "At first, we thought it was red ink from a leaky Stamper Pad. Upon further investigation, we discovered it tasted delicious."

"Ketchup *is* pretty delicious," Glizzy admitted.

"That may be so, but we have strict rules," Spex said. "Food and drinks can damage books, maps, and other important documents. This is why food is not permitted in the Library. One of you has broken that rule, and we demand punishment!"

Scoop rolled out of her hammock. "Let's get out of here," she whispered.

"What's the rush?" Slice asked.

"I have a feeling I know who Spex thinks came to the Library," she said.

Glizzy walked to the edge of the stove and looked down at Spex. "And who do you think got ketchup on the floor of the Library?"

Spex scanned the Cafeteria and finally pointed at Totz. "It was him," she said.

"And what makes you say it was Totz?" Glizzy asked.

"Because he has come into the Library at least four other times," Spex said.

"The only other ones in the Library have been Slice, Scoop, and Fry," Richard said.

"But ketchup doesn't pair well with pizza, ice cream, or donuts," Spex said. "Only tater tots. Seize him!"

"It wasn't me," Totz said. "I haven't been to the Library since we snuck in dressed as a thesaurus. And you saw me that day. No ketchup."

Scoop tugged on Totz's arm. "Let's go," she said.

"Let's run," Slice added.

Slice, Scoop, and Totz slid down a dishrag and ran. They scurried under a chair, around the legs of a few tables, and beneath the sink. Spex, Richard, and the stampers chased them.

"We can hide in Rasher's laboratory," Slice said. "The door is at the back of the Cooler."

"Maybe he can give us some gadgets to help us hide from Spex, too," Totz said. "At least until we sort this all out."

"Do we know the secret password?" Scoop said.

"We guessed it last time," Slice said. "Fingers crossed for another stroke of luck!"

They entered the Cooler and weaved around a few cartons until they reached the back. They slid aside a box of frozen hamburger patties and knocked.

No answer.

They knocked louder.

Still no answer.

"We know you're hiding in there!" Spex called into the Cooler. "Come out with your crispy hands up!"

Scoop pounded on the door again. "Rasher!" she yelled. "Let us in!"

Slice tapped Scoop on the cone. "Uh, maybe you should read this."

There was a note taped to the door.

"Why would a piece of bacon want to go fishing?!" Totz asked.

"Why would a tater tot want to learn to play the banjo?" Slice said.

"This is very bad timing!" Totz cried.

"I doubt Rasher thought Spex and Richard might come to the Cafeteria to accuse you of dripping ketchup on the Library floor before he went fishing," Scoop said.

"Then we have no choice," Totz said. His shoulders sagged and he walked out.

Spex, Richard, and the stampers were waiting for them at the door to the Cooler.

"That's more like it," Spex said. "Now please come with us to face your punishment."

"Hold on," Glizzy said. "We don't know for sure if Totz did what you say he did."

"There is no other explanation," Spex said. "He will come with us and face his punishment."

Slice and Scoop pushed their way to the front.

"Give us a chance to prove his innocence," Slice said.

"Actually, he's innocent until *proven* guilty," Scoop said. "Spex and the folks from the Library will have to *prove* he's guilty."

Richard's pages fluttered. "According to Statute 444, Section 12, Subsection 15c of the Belching Walrus Elementary

I Have NO Idea How I Knew That!

Code, he is innocent until proven guilty in a court of law," he said.

"Oh, we can prove he's guilty," Spex said. "We have witnesses, security camera footage, everything we need."

Richard's pages fluttered again. "According to Statute 444, Section 12, Subsection 22b of the Belching Walrus Elementary Code, he must also have a speedy trial."

"Does that mean we have to talk fast?" Slice said.

"I thought a spiedie was grilled chicken on a bun," Glizzy said. "It's popular in Binghamton, New York."

"Speedy, not spiedie," Spex said. "It means the trial needs to happen soon."

"Then the trial will be in two hours," Glizzy said.

"That doesn't give us much time," Slice said. "Scoop, Totz, and I will have to hurry."

"You and Scoop will have to hurry," Spex said. "Totz will stay with us until the trial."

"That's not fair!" Scoop said. "I thought he was innocent until proven guilty."

"HE IS A FLIGHT RISK," a voice boomed. It was Baron von Lineal, ruler of the Main Office. "Totz has a history of running away. It's too risky to have him roaming about Belching Walrus Elementary."

"It's just a little ketchup," Totz said. "I mean, it wasn't me who did it, but it was just some ketchup on the carpet."

"And what happens if we let this go?" Baron von Lineal asked. "Mustard in the Hallway? Barbecue sauce in the Science Room? Horseradish in the Gymnasium? Belching Walrus Elementary would be a condiment catastrophe!"

Baron von Lineal paced back and forth. "The trial will be in two hours in the Auditorium. Totz will be held on the stage. My decision is final."

NOM NOM NOM

WE'D LOVE SOME BBQ SAUCE IN THE SCIENCE ROOM!

Scoop tugged at Slice. "Let's go," she said. "There's no time to lose."

"Don't worry, Totz!" Slice called over his shoulder. "We'll get you out of this messy mess!"

But as they ran out of the Cafeteria, Slice wasn't so sure he believed it.

# CHAPTER 3

## In the Shadows and in the Library

**W**here are we going?" Slice asked as they ran down the Hallway.

"We'll start at the scene of the crime," Scoop said. "We need to see the mess."

"But we're not allowed in the Library," Slice said. "If we end up in trouble like Totz, who's left to help him?"

Scoop slowed. "You're right," she said. "But we

have to see the ketchup. Maybe it will give us some idea of who *did* go into the Library."

"I have an idea," Slice said. "Follow me."

Slice led Scoop around the corner and stopped at an air vent. "Maybe if we go through the ducts, we can see the ketchup from the vent that blows into the Library."

"Great idea," Scoop said. "Plus, the cool air will keep me from melting!"

They flipped open the vent and ran through the shiny silver ducts.

**Grooooooooaaaaannnn** . . .

Slice and Scoop stopped.

"What was that?" Slice asked.

"A groan," Scoop said.

"I know it was a groan," Slice said. "But what *made* the groan?"

They crept to the end of the duct and peeked around the corner.

Nothing.

They inched down the next duct and peeked around the corner.

Nothing.

"I guess it was nothing," Scoop said.

**Grooooooooaaaaannnn** . . .

This time the groan was louder, closer.

Slice turned to run the other way, but Scoop

stopped him. "We've got to keep going," she said. "For Totz."

Slice took a deep breath. "For Totz," he said.

They crept around the next corner and peeked through the closed vent.

The Library was quieter than usual. No pencils scribbled. No stampers stamped. Two large books stood silently guarding the door. Slice and Scoop could see the trail of ketchup clearly.

"It's a strange pattern," Scoop said. "Sort of like a dot and then a streak."

"Yeah," Slice said. "Those don't look like Totz's footprints at all."

"I need to get a closer look," Scoop said.

"We're not allowed down there," Slice said. "Plus, it looks like Spex has guards at the door. We wouldn't last two seconds before they sounded the alarm."

"Maybe we can't go to the ketchup," Scoop said, "but what if the ketchup came to us? Follow me."

# CHAPTER 3.1

## In the Slammer

**O**ne spotlight shone down from above the stage, lighting up a small hamster cage. Totz stood inside, holding the bars with his hands.

"So, where were you on the night of..." Spex paused to think. "Well, earlier tonight?"

"I already told you. I was having a painting lesson with Scoop," Totz said.

"Hah! A likely story," Spex said.

"Why would I want to go in the Library?" Totz said. "Every time I've been there, I've been chased out. One time, we got lost in the Maze of Shelves and almost got squashed by a huge book!"

"You'll have to excuse me for that," Richard said. "I was a bit overexcited."

Suddenly, the door flung open and the Auditorium filled with the scent of salty deliciousness.

"Flopping fishies!" It was Rasher, the slice of tasty bacon who lived in his laboratory at the back of the Cooler. "No more questions. I need a few minutes to speak with my client."

Spex began to argue, but Rasher cut her off. "According to Article 23, Section 153, Subsection 13c of the Belching Walrus Elementary Code, anyone accused of a crime has the right to a lawyer."

"You're an inventor, not a lawyer," Spex said.

Rasher held up a framed certificate. "I can do more than one thing," he said. "I recently graduated from the finest law school in Belching Walrus Elementary. It's in the Main Office."

Spex sighed and stomped out of the Auditorium. Richard followed her close behind.

After the door slammed shut, Rasher stood next to the hamster cage and sat down. "We have a lot of work to do,"

I NEVER STOP LEARNING!

he said. "The trial will be here before you know it."

# CHAPTER 4
## Cleanup in Aisle Library

**B**ack in the Hallway, Scoop climbed up a chair leg and onto a desk.

"What are we doing up here?" Slice asked.

"When there's a mess on the floor, who do you call?" Scoop asked.

"I don't call anyone," Slice said. "I don't mind it a little messy."

Scoop rolled her eyes and pressed the button on the intercom.

"THERE IS A MESS ON THE CARPET IN THE LIBRARY," Scoop said. Her voice echoed in every corner of Belching Walrus Elementary. "I REPEAT, THERE IS A MESS ON THE CARPET IN THE LIBRARY."

Suddenly, a door flew open and Mother Mop burst out, followed by her horde of cleaning supplies. There was a bucket filled with soapy water, a bunch of rags, and two spray bottles.

"Hide," Scoop said. "We don't want them to wipe us up, too."

Slice and Scoop ducked behind a box of rubber

bands as the cleaning supplies raced past them. They stormed into the Library and began to clean.

"Don't touch anything!" Spex hollered. "This is a crime scene!"

"This is a huge mess and it must be cleaned," Mother Mop said. "It is our life's mission. After all, what would happen if we didn't clean?"

"We'd all be happier?" Slice whispered.

Scoop shushed him. "We have to time this perfectly," she said.

"Time *what* perfectly?" Slice asked.

But Scoop ignored him. She was busy looping together rubber bands to make a long, stretchy chain.

After the cleaning supplies finished their job, they marched silently down the Hallway back to their Closet.

Mother Mop passed by Scoop and Slice. Her strings were stained red. A broom, three spray bottles, and a bucket followed her. Several rags were hanging out of the bucket, all stained red, too.

Scoop handed one end of the rubber band chain to Slice and looped the other end around her ankle. She looked off the edge of the desk and leaped.

It was a perfect swan dive. The chain of rubber

bands trailed behind her. When the slack ran out, the chain went taut and began to stretch, slowing Scoop's fall.

"Here we go, boys!" one rubber band said.

"Hold on tight!" another called out.

Before Scoop plopped onto the Hallway tile, the chain of rubber bands stretched to its limit. Scoop came to a brief stop just above the bucket and grabbed one of the rags. Then she shot back up to the desktop.

Scoop landed next to Slice and rolled behind the box of rubber bands. Slice crouched beside her as the rest of the cleaning supplies continued toward the Closet.

When the door finally closed, Scoop and Slice turned to the rag.

"What's your name?" Scoop said.

"I don't gotta tell you nothin'," the rag said. He was stained red from his recent work.

"Look, we can do this the easy way or we can do it the hard way," Slice said.

"What's the hard way?" the rag asked.

"I . . . uh . . . I'm not sure," Slice said. "It's just something folks say."

"We don't mean you any harm," Scoop said. "We just need to figure out what happened in the Library."

"You ragnapped me!" the rag said. "I was just

doin' my job, tired from a long five minutes of work, and what happens next? I'm snatched from my bucket like a feather duster grabbin' a dust mite."

"Yeah, we're sorry about that," Scoop said, "but our friend is being blamed for that mess. We need to prove he's innocent."

"My name's Wipe-a-licious," the rag said. "I've done cleanups in every room in this school. I've wiped up paint in the Art Room. I've cleaned up soup in the Cafeteria and ink in the Main Office. I've even wiped up bunny barf in the Science Room."

I THOUGHT WE AGREED NEVER TO MENTION THAT AGAIN??

"We need a sample of what you just wiped up in the Library," Slice said.

"What, the ketchup?" Wipe-a-licious said. "It was delicious."

45

"So, it *was* ketchup?" Scoop said.

"One hundred percent pure ketchup," Wipe-a-licious said. "Tomatoes, white vinegar, sugar, spices, and a hint of sodium benzoate. Tastes much better than the dust and slop we usually eat."

Scoop dipped her finger into the red liquid and tasted it. "Ketchup and some cleanser."

"That's not just *any* cleanser," Wipe-a-licious said. "That's a 2019 Sani-Clean Spray. Mother Mop insists we only use the best. Now, if you'll excuse me. I've gotta go."

Wipe-a-licious scurried down the desk leg and flopped down the Hallway. Before Slice and Scoop had a chance to figure out what to do next, the door to the Supply Closet burst open. Mother

DON'T EVER SUCK FLOOR KETCHUP OFF A DIRTY RAG!

Mop, a bucket, two spray bottles, and an army of rags clattered out.

"They're over there!" Wipe-a-licious said. "Food in the Hallway!"

Slice and Scoop ran.

# CHAPTER 4.1

## Order in the Court!

**T**he Auditorium was filled with folks from all over the school. On the stage, Rasher and Totz sat at one table. Spex and Richard sat at another. In front of them, Baron von Lineal sat at a tall desk, towering over everyone. He banged his gavel three times.

"Order in the court!" Baron von Lineal said. "The trial of the Library versus Totz will begin. Bring in the jury."

A group of eight marched into the Auditorium. They were from every room in Belching Walrus Elementary (all the rooms except the Library or the Cafeteria). There was Chip from the Tech Room, Bounce the tennis ball from the Gymnasium, Clip the paper

A GAVEL IS A FANCY HAMMER...

clip from the Main Office, Drum from the Music Room, François the paintbrush and Black Crayon from the Art Room, Boo-Boo the bandage from the Nurse's Office, and Houdini the hamster from the Science Room.

"Let's start with opening statements," Baron von Lineal said. "The Library goes first."

Spex got up and began pacing back and forth in front of the stand. "Ketchup. It is the stainiest of

all the condiments," she began. "Ketchup tracked across the clean carpet of the Library? Not okay! We have strict rules banning food from the Library. It gets on our pages. It stains our dust jackets. It destroys the order and cleanliness we work so hard to keep."

Spex moved closer to the jury. "During this trial, we will show you how Totz was the one who broke our rules. We will show you how he tracked ketchup across our clean carpet, which had to be deep cleaned and sterilized. We will show you how he put the Library and the whole school—each and every one of us—at risk!" Spex paused. "Thank you."

Spex wiped a tear from her lens and sat down.

A murmur spread through the courtroom.

Baron von Lineal banged his gavel. "Order in the court!" he barked. "Rasher, you are defending Totz in this trial. Do you want to make an opening statement?"

"Spinning sardines, of course I do!" Rasher said. He patted Totz on the arm, stood up, and cleared his throat. "All that stuff Spex just said . . . it's hogwash. Thank you."

Rasher sat back down.

Totz gulped.

# CHAPTER 5

## The Plot and the Ketchup Thicken

**S**lice and Scoop ran down the Hallway. They turned a corner and bolted down another. The cleaning supplies, headed by Mother Mop, chased close behind, skidding into one wall and then another. Water sloshed out of the bucket. Clean white rags hooted and hollered.

Scoop scurried up a chair, climbed onto a table,

and pushed the button on the intercom. "Close your doors!" she hollered. "Cleaning supplies on the loose!"

Doors started slamming shut up and down the Hallway.

"Now where do we go?" Slice said. "All the doors are locked!"

"There will be one door left open," Scoop said. "Follow me."

They skidded around one last turn and Scoop led Slice to the Cleaning Supply Closet.

The door stood wide open and the air smelled of cleansers and musty mops.

"I'm not going in there," Slice said. "We'll be trapped!"

"It's better to be safe in there than unsafe out here," Scoop said.

The cleaning supplies came around the corner. Their hooting and hollering grew louder as they drew near.

"There is no escape!" Mother Mop said. "We're going to mop you up!"

Just before Mother Mop and the cleaning horde reached them, Slice and Scoop dove into the Closet and pulled the door shut.

## THWAP, THWAP, PLOP, SLAP!!!

Rags, brooms, and mops slapped into the door, but Slice and Scoop were safe. They sank to the floor to catch their breath.

"We know you're in there," a rag called out from the other side of the door.

"We can smell your scrumptious cheese and your messy, drippy ice cream," another said.

"I'm not messy and drippy," Scoop said.

Slice looked at her in concern. "Now what?"

"Let's look around," Scoop said.

They walked along the tall shelves.

## THUMP, THWIP-THWAP, THUMP, SLAP!!!

The banging on the door grew louder.

"We can smell your crispy deliciousness!" a voice hissed.

"Here, look . . ." Scoop said. She knelt on the ground and pointed.

"A dot of red," Slice said. "More ketchup. So what?"

Scoop touched the dot with her finger and tasted it. "Not ketchup," she said. "Red paint. When paint dries, it gets flaky and stays bright red. When ketchup dries, it stays sticky and turns dark red. This is paint."

"Are you sure?" Slice said.

"I work with paint every day," Scoop said. "I know what it feels like. I know what it smells like. I know how it dries. This is red paint."

**GROOOOOOOOAAAAANNNN . . .**

A groan echoed through the Cleaning Supply Closet.

"I'll bet my chocolate scoop that the groaning has something to do with the ketchup tracks in the Library," Scoop said.

"But those groans sound scary!" Slice said.

**THUMP, THWAPPITY, THUMP, THW—**

The thumping stopped.

Scoop and Slice looked at each other.

"Where did they go?" Scoop asked.

"Maybe on a long vacation to Sub-Basement 3," Slice said.

Scoop put her ear to the door. "Not a peep," she said. "When the groaning started, the cleaning supplies seem to have disappeared. Odd. I think they're gone."

"There's only one way to find out," Slice said. He opened the door and peeked out.

The Hallway was empty.

Scoop stepped out of the Cleaning Supply Closet. "Let's go," she said.

"Where now?"

"I have no idea," Scoop said. "We'll figure it out on the way."

# CHAPTER 5.1
## Witness for the Prosecution

**S**o, you say you saw Totz walk across the carpet with your own two eyes?" Rasher asked a young children's book named Alice.

Alice pushed up her glasses and nodded.

"I need you to say yes or no, please," Rasher said.

"Um . . . yes . . ." Alice whispered.

"Please speak so everyone can hear you," Rasher said.

So...

"Yes," Alice said louder.

Rasher paced back and forth, his hands clasped behind his crispy back. "And can you describe exactly what you saw?"

"Um . . . um . . . I was on my shelf . . ."

"Louder, please," Rasher said.

Alice straightened in her chair. "I was on my shelf taking my daily nap," she said. "That's when I heard the sound. It woke me up. It was a thump and then a sliding sound. Like *thump, slide, thump, slide.* Over and over again. I saw a shadowy figure walking across the carpet. They were leaving a messy trail of ketchup behind."

"And do you see that shadowy figure in this courtroom today?" Rasher asked.

Alice nodded.

"I need you to say yes or no," Rasher reminded her.

"Yes," Alice said.

"Please point him out to us."

Alice pointed at Totz. "It was him!" she said, trembling.

A gasp spread through the courtroom.

Baron von Lineal banged his gavel a bunch of times and the room went silent.

Rasher stepped closer to Alice. "Were you wearing your glasses during your nap, Alice?"

"No, sir," she said. "I always put on my headphones, turn on 'Sounds of a Rolling Book Cart,' and take off my glasses before I go to sleep."

"Can you take off your glasses now, please?"

"I object!" Spex said. "She needs her glasses to ssss... She needs her glasses to safely walk around the room."

OBJECTION MEANS YOU DON'T THINK THE QUESTION IS FAIR...

"Objection overruled," Baron von Lineal said. He

turned to Alice. "Please take off your glasses."

Alice removed her glasses. Her eyes were so squinty you could barely see them on her illustrated cover.

"Now, can you point at the one you saw in the Library who made the tracks across the carpet?" Rasher asked.

Alice pointed at the chair where Totz had

been sitting, but no one was there... No one was there because Totz had moved to another seat.

A gasp spread across the courtroom.

"No more questions," Rasher said.

# CHAPTER 6
## Searching, Searching, Searching

**Scoop and Slice** searched as far as the farthest classrooms in Belching Walrus Elementary, but everything looked like it always did. Even the folks they talked to had not seen anything out of the ordinary.

As they passed the Nurse's Office, Fry opened the door. "Is it all clear?" he asked.

"The cleaning supplies have disappeared," Slice said. "How is medical school going?"

DUCKY SHOOK HIS HEAD...

COACH TWEETED...

BLU1 + GREEN1 WHIRRED...

MAGIC MARKER'S CAP TWISTED...

"It's so interesting," Fry said. "Want to come in for a tour?"

"Sorry, we really don't have much time," Scoop said. "We're trying to save Totz."

THE MORE YOU KNOW, THE MORE YOU KNOW WHAT YOU **DON'T** KNOW?!

"Okay," Fry said. "I need to get back anyhow. We are trying to reverse the aging process in food."

"You can do that?" Slice said.

"You know Rasher's Stay-Fresh-o-Lator?" Fry said.

"It helps keep food fresh," Scoop said.

Fry nodded. "We are taking it a step further to restore food that has already expired."

"I thought when food spoils, it spoils," Slice said.

"Don't be so sure," Fry said, smiling.

"Well, that sounds incredible," Scoop said. "Good luck. It's great to see you!"

"Yeah," Slice agreed. "Good luck!"

Fry shut the door, and Slice and Scoop returned to their search. Finally, they came back to where they'd started.

"This is useless," Slice said. "We're running in circles while Totz is fighting for his life."

"There has to be something we've overlooked," Scoop said. "What do we know so far?"

Slice thought about it. "We know there were tracks left in the Library and that those tracks were made of ketchup."

"We also know that there has been spooky groaning around the school," Scoop said.

"And that the cleaning supplies run to that groaning," Slice added.

1. TRACKS IN LIBRARY...
2. SPOOKY GROANING...
3. CLEANING SUPPLIES RUNNING AROUND...
ALSO: DON'T FORGET TO BRUSH TEETH...

Scoop scratched her vanilla scoop. "Maybe we need to find where the groaning is coming from," she said.

"We first heard it in the air ducts," Slice said. He went to the nearest one and started to open it. "Wait, what's this?"

Scoop peered over Slice's shoulder. There were red smudges on the vent.

"Ketchup!" Scoop said.

"Not red paint?" Slice asked.

"Nope," Scoop said. "I know high-fructose corn syrup when I see it."

They opened the air vent and peered inside.

Suddenly, a pair of green hands reached out and pulled them in.

Grooooooan!

It was a half loaf of bread. But this was not just any half loaf of bread. This half loaf of bread was covered in cobwebs. His crust was coated in a grayish-green fuzz, and he stank, a little sour and rotten. Next to him stood a stalk of celery so wilted that she flopped over. Her leaves were wrinkled and gray.

"You . . . will . . . join us," the loaf of bread said.

"It's the undead zombie monsters from behind the stove!" Slice screamed.

"Run!" Scoop cried out.

They ran down the air duct and made a turn. Two crusty green french fries shuffled closer, their arms reaching out. *"Grooooooan!"*

They ran down another duct and made two more turns. A half-eaten, moldy peach crawled toward them.

*"Grooooan!* You . . . will . . . join us . . ."

They slid down a chute and ran down another tunnel. All the while, they heard sounds behind them . . . *Stomp-sliiide, stomp-sliiide, stomp-sliiide.*

Slice pulled on an air vent. It swung open and they hopped through. They were in the Science Room. Napoleon, Miss Bun-Bun, and the rest of the Science Room crew were hanging out. Daisy the ferret stirred in her cage.

"And to what do we owe the pleasure of this visit?" Napoleon the chick said.

"We are right in the middle of our game of Duck, Duck, Goose," Shelly the turtle added.

"We're being chased!" Scoop panted.

"When are you *not* being chasssed?" Slither the snake asked.

Slice looked down at his hands. Right where the undead half loaf of bread had grabbed him was covered in a grayish-green fuzz.

He turned to his friends and showed them. "It might be too late!"

The room grew very quiet.

# CHAPTER 6.1

## Video Proof

**T**otz squirmed in his seat. He wasn't very good at sitting still for long periods of time. Sitting in the hamster cage for hours was tough enough. He wanted to be under the utility sink talking with Slice and Scoop. He wanted to be in the Cooler writing rhymes. He wanted to be in the Music Room strumming his banjo. Anywhere but here.

The jury looked tired, too. Drum rolled his

eyes. Bounce hopped in his chair. Black Crayon was coloring.

"We're almost done," Rasher said to Totz. "They have no proof. It's all *'He said, tater tot said.'* They can't prove you were at the scene of the crime. They can't prove you were covered in ketchup. The carpet has been cleaned, so there was no damage. It's almost over."

But Totz wasn't so sure. He had never seen a trial before and didn't know the rules. All he knew was that Baron von Lineal had never been very nice, and now he was the one holding the gavel.

Richard crossed the courtroom. "I will be questioning the next witness," he announced.

"This is highly unusual," Baron von Lineal said. "The head lawyer questions witnesses."

Richard's pages ruffled. "How can Spex question the witness if Spex *is* the witness?"

A murmur spread throughout the Auditorium.

Baron von Lineal banged his gavel. "Order in the court," he said.

Spex walked across the Auditorium stage and sat in the seat next to Baron von Lineal while a team from the Tech Room rolled a video monitor onto the stage.

"I object!" Rasher said. "No one mentioned anything about a video monitor."

"Your Honor," Richard said. "We have *proof* that Totz is the one who left the trail of ketchup across the Library."

Baron von Lineal seemed to like being called "Your Honor." He straightened in his seat and said, "I will allow this new evidence."

Richard paced back and forth in front of Spex. "So, is it true there is video proof Totz left the trail of ketchup in the Library?"

"That is correct," Spex said.

"And why do you have video proof?" Richard asked.

Spex crossed her arms. "Because we have a 'no food in the Library' policy, yet Totz and his friends always go there. They fled the cleaning supplies in the Library. They dressed up as a thesaurus to get a map from the School Archives. They even spy on us through the air vents! I needed to do *something* before they got their greasy hands all over our precious pages!"

"And can we see this video?" Richard asked.

"I thought you'd never ask." Spex turned her lenses toward the monitor.

The black-and-white video was filmed from the far corner of the Library. They could see shelves and the front counter along with some tables and chairs. The time ticked by across the bottom of the screen as the video rolled. Suddenly, a short, rectangular figure loped across the carpet. With each footstep, it left a dark stain behind it.

"Pause the video," Richard said. "Zoom in."

The video paused and the monitor zoomed in on the figure.

"That is not me," Totz whispered to Rasher.

"It looks an awful lot like you," Rasher said. "This is a problem."

# CHAPTER 7
## The Sickness Spreads

**W**ithin minutes, the grayish-green fuzz had spread. It had worked its way over Slice's hands and up his arms to his shoulders.

"What's happening to me?" he asked.

The animals of the Science Room shied away, but Scoop looked closely.

"It looks like some kind of growth," she said. "And it's spreading fast."

"He smells distasteful," Napoleon said.

"That's rude," Miss Bun-Bun said. "They're our guests."

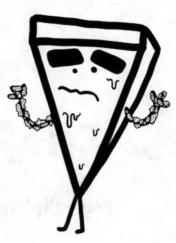

"They are *not* our guests," Napoleon said. "They barged in through the air vent in the middle of our nice game of Duck, Duck, Goose. And the cheesy one smells distasteful."

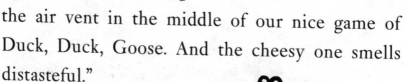

Napoleon turned to Slice and Scoop. "I'm going to have to ask you to leave," she said. "We would love to help, but I've got to protect the Science Room."

Shelly coughed. "I am

very sensitive . . . to unusual smells and grayish-green fuzz."

"We helped *you* when Daisy the ferret was on the loose," Scoop said.

"And we appreciate that," Napoleon said. "You are very good at running around in the air ducts and you saved us. However, we are not good at curing diseases, and this looks very much like a disease. You may go back through the vent or leave through the door."

"Er, we'll go through the door," Slice said. He didn't want to run into that half loaf of bread, that stalk of celery, or those french fries again.

"This is the last thing we need," Scoop said. "Totz is fighting for his life in the Auditorium and now we have to figure out what's going on with you."

Slice looked at his arms again. The grayish-green fuzz was spreading across his cheesy chest.

"I don't feel so well," Slice said. He dropped to his knees.

"Come on," Scoop said, helping him up. "We have to get you to the Nurse's Office, okay?"

But Slice didn't answer. The only word that came out of his mouth was *"Grooooooan!"*

Startled, Scoop leaped back.

Slice's eyes were sunken and his head lolled over to one side at a strange angle. His arms were raised and he was covered from crust to tip in grayish-green fuzz.

*"Grooooooan!"* he said again.

Scoop grabbed Slice and pulled him down the Hallway. Luckily, the Nurse's Office wasn't far away.

# CHAPTER 7.1
## Totz Caught Red-Handed

**S**pex flipped through some papers on her table. "So, you admit to coming into the Library to escape the cleaning supplies?" she asked Totz.

"Yes, but we had to—"

"A simple yes or no will do," Spex said, cutting Totz off.

"Yes," Totz said. He hated just saying yes because he had an excuse for that. They were running for their lives!

"And you admit that you snuck into the Library disguised as a thesaurus to look at a map of the school?" Spex said.

"If we hadn't come there—"

"A simple yes or no will do," Spex said again.

"Er, yes," Totz said.

Spex walked across the courtroom and rested her arms on the sides of Totz's chair. "And what is the most common condiment paired with tater tots?"

"Um . . . ketchup?" he said.

"KETCHUP!" Spex barked.

"Ketchup goes on plenty of other foods," Totz said.

"And can you please hold up your hands?" Spex asked Totz.

Totz held up his hands.

"Aha!" Spex said. "Right there for all you folks to see . . . KETCHUP!"

Totz looked at his hands. They were covered in red.

"Caught red-handed!" Spex said.

A shocked murmur spread across the courtroom.

Totz's shoulders sagged. He wished Slice and Scoop were there.

# CHAPTER 8

## Code Yummy

**F**ry snapped on a pair of gloves and put a surgical mask over his face as they ran across the Nurse's Office. Slice was strapped to a rolling bed pushed by two tongue depressors.

"Right this way!" Fry called out. "Code yummy! Code yummy!"

"There's nothing yummy about this," Scoop said, pointing to the fuzz still growing on Slice's

body. It had spread to his legs and across most of his face.

*"Grooooooan!"* Slice said.

"No, code yummy means there is a medical emergency for food," Fry explained. "Code staple is for office supplies. Code cuteness is for the class pets. Code racquet is for the Gymnasium. You wouldn't believe how many medical emergencies we see from there. Coach works them hard."

Scoop was impressed with how confident Fry seemed, like seeing Slice strapped to a table and covered in stinky, grayish-green fuzz was nothing to worry about. They rolled Slice into a white room with bright lights. Rolls

NO PAIN = NO GAIN!!

of bandages, a pair of tweezers, a thermometer, and a stethoscope clustered around the bed and started working.

"Why didn't I get sick?" Scoop asked.

"This type of mold doesn't grow on ice cream," Fry said. "There is only one way to save Slice, but it's a new treatment."

"It works, though, right?" Scoop asked.

Fry thought about how to answer the question. He decided the truth was best. "It's never worked before," he said. "Baked potato ended up mashed. Banana ended up baby food. Tomato ended up diced. But I've fixed the process. I know how to do this."

> I WAS ALWAYS BABY FOOD, I JUST DIDN'T KNOW IT!

BABY FOOD

"I'm not so sure this is a good idea," Scoop said.

"Trust me," Fry said. "It might take a little time, but I know I can cure him."

"Time is something we do *not* have," Scoop said. "Totz is on trial and there are moldy zombies running around Belching Walrus Elementary!"

> I'M CURED!

"I'll do my best," Fry said.

Slice thrashed against the straps across his chest. His eyes rolled back. *"Grooooooan!"*

Scoop found the nearest air vent. She knew the mystery in the Library was somehow connected to the food zombies. If she was immune to the grayish-green fuzz, she had to see if they could help.

*"Grooooooan!"*

Scoop ran down one duct and then down another.

The trouble was that the groaning echoed all around her. She didn't know which way to go.

"*Grooooooan!*"

She turned again and ran right into the half loaf of bread. She bounced off him and fell to the ground.

Within moments, she was surrounded by grayish-green french fries, grayish-green cheese, a grayish-green chicken leg, and a bunch of grayish-green grapes. The stench was overpowering, but Scoop stood and faced them.

"*Grooooooan!*" the grayish-green food said. "You . . . will . . . join us . . ."

"J-J-Join you?" Scoop stammered. "M-My name is Scoop and I need your help. I might be able to help you, too."

The half loaf of bread loomed over her. "*Grooooooan!*" He coughed and cleared his throat. "Sorry, we've been groaning so long it's hard to get out proper words."

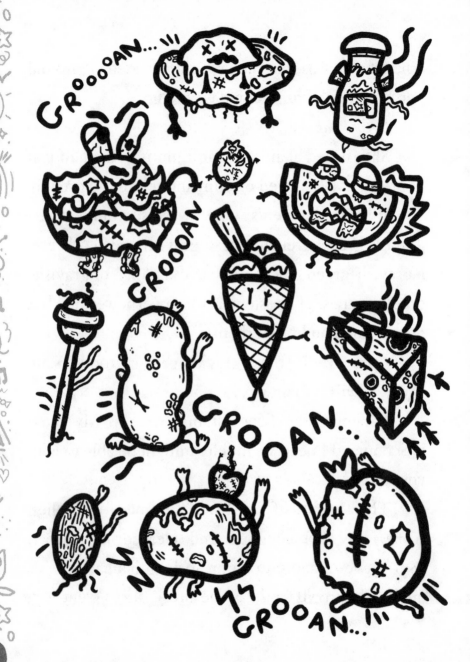

GROOOAN...

GROOOAN

GROOAN...

GROOAN...

The half loaf of bread helped Scoop up. "My name is Regimold," he said.

"Nice to meet you," Scoop said. "I thought I already knew all the food at Belching Walrus Elementary."

Regimold looked down at his hands. "I wasn't always like this," he said. "None of us were. You know that spooky story Glizzy tells around the campfire to scare the young ones?"

"You mean his cautionary tale about getting too close to the back of the Freezer?" Scoop asked.

"That story is true," Regimold said. "I was named Reginald. I had the best singing voice in all of the Cafeteria. I never paid much mind to Glizzy's stories and wanted to show off in front of my friends. I went to the back of the Freezer and looked down there."

"What happened?" Scoop asked.

"I got too close to the edge and before I knew it, I fell," Regimold said. "Some bread slices went left,

some went right. The mold sickness set in quickly, and I was left how you see me now. Other food soon followed. Since then, we've lived our lives in hiding."

"Who are you hiding from?" Scoop asked. "Why wouldn't you just come to us for help?"

"We don't want to allow our mold sickness to spread to any of the other food," Regimold said. "Anyhow, we're being hunted. They lure us out and pick us off one by one."

"Who is hunting you?" Scoop asked.

"The cleaning sup- plies," Regimold explained. "They lure us out into the open with the most beauti- ful groaning. When we go out to join them . . . WHAP! Down comes a mop or a broom or a cleaning rag."

Scoop didn't know

what to say. In moments like this, Scoop or Totz would usually jump in with a joke or a rhyme to lighten the mood.

"Why . . . uh . . . why are you groaning in the first place?" Scoop asked.

"It's our choir," Regimold said. "Don't you enjoy our music?"

Suddenly, a group of grayish-green food

clustered together and belted out the loudest groan of all.

Scoop wanted to hold her ears from the terrible sound, but she thought that might be rude. "It's . . . uh . . . lovely," she said.

"You don't care for it," Regimold said. "You think we're terrible."

"It's not that," Scoop explained. "My friends are in trouble. I thought you might be able to help."

# CHAPTER 8.1
## The Prosecution Rests

**I don't know** what to do," Rasher said to Totz during a break. "I believe you when you say you did not go into the Library, but all the evidence points to you."

Totz did not know what to do, either. He had only gone into the Library when it was necessary. The Maze of Shelves was terrifying, The books he had met were always grumpy. Even Compass Rose in the School Archives seemed to always be complaining.

Totz looked around the courtroom. Baron von Lineal was measuring his gavel. Spex was focusing on her paperwork. Everyone else was whispering to one another.

Finally, the jury filed back into the courtroom and took their seats.

Baron von Lineal banged his gavel. "Everyone please be quiet," he said.

A hush spread through the courtroom.

"It is time to hear from the jury," Baron von Lineal said. He turned to the jury box. "Have you reached a verdict?"

Chip from the Tech Room stood. "We have, Your Honor."

"And what is your verdict?" Baron von Lineal asked.

Chip unfolded a small slip of paper and read from it. "In the count of trespassing in the first degree and getting messy ketchup on the carpet in the second degree, we find the defendant, Totz the tater tot, guil—"

"STOP RIGHT THERE!"

It was Scoop. She had burst through the
Auditorium doors and was running down the center aisle. Regimold and the rest of the grayish-green
zombie food limped in behind her.

"I have new evidence." Scoop panted. "Totz is
innocent and I can prove it!"

# CHAPTER 8.2

## Recovery Time

**S**lice heard a beeping sound. He opened his eyes. A light shone down into his face. He tried to look around, but everything looked blurry. Someone rubbed his arm to comfort him.

"It's okay," Fry said.

"Where am I?" Slice asked.

"You're in the Nurse's Office," Fry said. "Your surgery went well."

"Thank goodness," a tiny voice said.

"Surgery?" Slice asked.

"You had mold sickness," Fry explained. "*Aspergillus*. Very aggressive."

"Why can't I see well?" Slice asked.

Fry pressed a button on a machine. "You are wrapped in Rasher's Stay-Fresh-o-Lator."

"It will help keep you fresh," the tiny voice said.

"Our cure paired with Rasher's Stay-Fresh-o-Lator," Fry said. "It saved you."

"Where is Scoop?" Slice asked. "Where is Totz?"

"Scoop had to leave," Fry said. "Something about Totz being on trial."

It all came back to Slice. They had been running through the air ducts trying to solve the mystery in the Library when he was grabbed by that scary bread monster. The grayish-green fuzz had spread across his body. They were kicked out of the Science Room. But that was the last he remembered.

Slice tore the plastic wrap from his face and leaped out of bed. He felt weak, but he rose to his feet.

"Aspergillus is a very aggressive mold," Fry said. "You need to rest."

"Rest is best," the tiny voice said.

Slice looked down to see a small tater tot looking up at him.

"Who are you?" Slice asked.

"I'm Tootie," the tater tot said. "Totz's distant cousin. I'm a doctor, just like Fry."

"The best food doctor there is," Fry said. "We are in medical school together."

"I'm more of a researcher," Tootie said. "I learn about food sicknesses and like to come up with ways to cure them."

"She's been helping us with the cure that saved you," Fry said.

"Once I thought about it, the solution was simple," Tootie said. "It all has to do with ketchup."

"Ketchup?" Slice asked.

"I asked myself why ketchup stays fresh so long while tomatoes seem to grow old more quickly," Tootie explained.

IT'S RUDE TO TALK ABOUT SOMEONE'S AGE...

Slice had tomatoes in his sauce, so he knew exactly what Tootie was getting at.

"After a little research, I discovered it had to do with *sodium benzoate*," Tootie said.

"Those are some long words," Slice said. "And I don't know what this has to do with—"

Tootie cut him off. "Sodium benzoate prevents food from spoiling," she said. "It protects us from bacteria, yeasts, and molds. I figured if I could combine the sodium benzoate with Rasher's

Stay-Fresh-o-Lator, maybe we could cure the disease that infected you."

"Thanks for your help," Slice said to Tootie. "Now, Scoop and Totz need *my* help."

"Nice to meet you," Tootie said. "Take some Stay-Fresh-o-Lator with you. You'll need to apply it every—"

But it was too late. Slice had already run out the door. Fry and Tootie gathered a few things and chased after him.

# CHAPTER 9

## Order in the Court!

**O**rder in the court! Order in the court!" Baron von Lineal hollered. "We will have no interruptions. The jury was just about to tell us if Totz is guilty or not guilty!"

"You can't decide if Totz is guilty or not guilty without *all* the evidence," Scoop said, marching down the center aisle. "That would not be very fair."

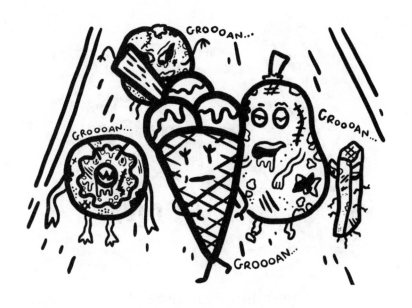

"This is about justice," Baron von Lineal said. "Not about being fair."

An unhappy murmur spread through the courtroom. Even Regimold and the grayish-green zombie food were confused.

Scoop climbed onto the stage and approached Baron von Lineal.

"Your Honor, we believe there is more going on than meets the eye," Scoop said. "Or the camera."

Another murmur spread through the Auditorium. And this murmur sounded excited.

"I object!" Spex cried out. "Totz is right there on the video. It's an open-and-shut case! I object, object, object!"

"I do like when someone calls me 'Your Honor,'"

Baron von Lineal said. "I will allow Scoop to speak."

Scoop began to pace. She finally stopped at the monitor and looked at the screen closely. "It does look like Totz was walking across the carpet in the Library, doesn't it?"

"Exactly!" Spex said.

"And ketchup," Scoop said. "Well, that pairs very nicely with tater tots, doesn't it?"

"We go well with everything!" a ketchup packet in the Auditorium cried out.

"So, how do we explain what we see in this video when I know Totz wasn't in the Library at all?" Scoop said. "When I know he was in art class with me?"

Scoop paused. The Auditorium was silent, not a single murmur. Scoop let the silence grow longer.

"Let me show you something," Scoop said. She pulled out Totz's painting. "It only had one tiny tater tot pictured in the corner."

"It's an unfinished painting," Spex said. "So what?"

"It's not just an unfinished painting. It is an unfinished *family portrait*," Scoop explained. "Totz only had the chance to paint one of his family members, but if you look closely, he had sketched

the rest of his family lightly in pencil. It's called 'blocking in.' It's a technique painters use to make sure everyone will fit on the canvas before they start."

"This doesn't prove anything," Spex said.

Scoop smiled. "It proves Totz isn't the only tater tot at Belching Walrus Elementary," she said. "Just because Totz went into the Library in the past doesn't mean he was the one who tracked ketchup on the carpet. Maybe Totz isn't the tater tot you are looking for."

Spex crossed her arms. "This doesn't mean Totz *didn't* do it," she said. "What about the ketchup on his hands?"

Scoop crossed the courtroom to where Totz and Rasher were

sitting. "Totz, can you please show us your hands?" she asked.

Totz held up his hands. They still had red on them.

"Ha!" Spex said. "Case closed. We caught him red-handed!"

"You really should wash up better," Scoop said to Totz. "But this time, I'm glad you didn't."

"You're glad he didn't wash his hands?" Baron von Lineal said. "The ketchup is still on his fingers!"

WHO ARE YOU CALLING DARK AND STICKY?!

Scoop turned to Baron von Lineal and the jury. "I'm glad he didn't wash up well because this is not ketchup at all. It's red paint—the same red paint that Totz used on his painting."

A murmur spread around the Auditorium.

"It is something I noticed in the Cleaning Supply Closet," Scoop explained. "When red paint dries, it stays red and gets flaky. When ketchup dries, it turns dark and sticky."

Scoop turned to Spex, then to the whole

Auditorium. "The stuff on Totz's hands is bright red and flaky."

Spex stood. "Then who is on that video?" she asked. "Who tracked ketchup across our perfectly clean carpet?"

Scoop walked to the edge of the Auditorium stage. She saw folks from every room in Belching Walrus Elementary—from the Cafeteria, the Gymnasium,

the Library, the Main Office, the Science Room, the Tech Room, the Art Room, the Nurse's Office, and the Music Room. There were folks from every room except one.

"I call to the stand Wipe-a-licious, the cleaning rag!" Scoop called out.

# CHAPTER 9.1
## Surprise Witness #1

I ain't tellin' you nothin'!" Wipe-a-licious said from his seat next to Baron von Lineal. "I got rights, you know!"

"It's true. You have rights," Scoop said. "Maybe you'd like to think about them for a while in the washing machine?"

Wipe-a-licious looked around the Auditorium. Finally, his raggy shoulders sagged. "A few days ago,

one of us—I think it
was Scrubby Bubbly—
figured out that if we
groaned in the Hallway,
food would come look-
ing for us. And we'd get
to clean it up."

"And why would
that matter to the clean-
ing supplies?" Scoop asked.

"Food, even moldy food, is much tastier than the
other things we clean up here at Belching Walrus
Elementary," Wipe-a-licious explained. "Dust and
broken crayons and bent paper clips don't taste very
good at all."

"So, you were luring innocent food out into the
Hallway so you could eat us?" Scoop asked.

Wipe-a-licious shrugged. "Hey, you can't blame
a guy for trying."

"Yes," Scoop said. "Yes, you can."

"Hey, can I get outta here?" Wipe-a-licious asked. "I hear there's a mess in the Gymnasium. A lot of yummy sweat."

Scoop thought about what Wipe-a-licious had told her. "No more questions," she said. "I call to the stand Regimold, the moldy half loaf of bread!"

# CHAPTER 9.2

## Surprise Witness #2

**W**hispers spread among the food in the Auditorium. They had never seen moldy bread before. Glizzy had not been lying about his campfire stories, and there was renewed excitement around his cautionary tales.

Scoop ignored the whispers and leaned in to hear Regimold answer her question.

"We usually just hang out behind the Freezer," Regimold said from the seat next to Baron von Lineal.

"We hang out and practice our singing. That is, we *used to* practice our singing . . ."

"What happened?" Scoop asked.

"We started to hear singing coming from the Hallway," Regimold said.

"Can you describe the singing?" Scoop asked.

"It sounded like this . . ." Regimold let out a low groan.

## GROOOOOAN! GROOOOOAN! GROOOOOAN!

Scoop held her ears and an unpleasant murmur spread across the Auditorium.

"It was beautiful," Regimold said. "We had to add that sound to our choir."

"What happened next?" Scoop asked.

A grayish-green tear trickled down Regimold's face. "Anyone who went out never returned."

Scoop pointed at the monitor that showed the blurry tater tot.

"And those footsteps . . ."

Scoop said. "That trail of ketchup. Do you see how there is a dot of ketchup and then a long streak of ketchup? What can you tell us about that?"

Regimold peered closely at the monitor. "It looks like a zombie walk to me," he said. "We all walk that way, with a stomp-sliiide."

"So, is it possible that this is not Totz on the video, but a moldy morsel of zombie food?" Scoop asked, pointing at the blurry figure on the screen.

Regimold shook his head. "I'm afraid not," he said.

"Why not?" she asked.

"Because we've never had a tater tot join us," Regimold explained. "No matter how cute and tiny they are, no matter how they roll when they fall down, a tater tot has never fallen behind the Freezer. Ever."

Scoop was sure her explanation was going to be right. She was sure Regimold would prove that

Totz was innocent. She looked across the court-room at Totz. She could see the worry on his face. She could also see something else on his face. It was grayish-green.

"Mold," Scoop said.

"Excuse me, young lady?" Baron von Lineal asked.

She pointed at Totz, then at Rasher. "Mold!"

Suddenly, the food in the Auditorium stood up and started screaming. They were covered in grayish-green mold. The mold had infected them all!

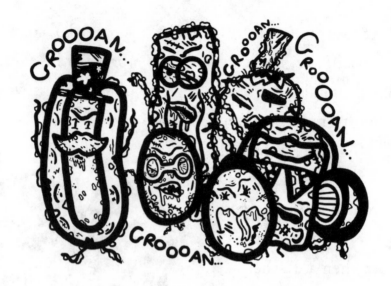

# CHAPTER 10
## Sodium Benzoate +
## Stay-Fresh-o-Lator

**T**he door to the Auditorium swung open.

"Everyone please settle down!" a voice boomed. It was Slice. He was wrapped in Stay-Fresh-o-Lator and carrying a small pail. Behind him stood Fry and Tootie holding rolls of plastic wrap. They were wrapped in Stay-Fresh-o-Lator, too.

Baron von Lineal banged his gavel. "ORDER IN

THE COURT!" he hollered. "THIS IS AGAINST ALL THE RULES!"

Rasher pounded his fist on the table. "Spectacular spores!" he cried out. "My Stay-Fresh-o-Lator!"

"Everyone stay in your seats," Tootie said. "This will only take a minute."

"But we're covered in mold!" Red the apple said.

"My delicious, crunchy crust is forever grayish-green and goopy!" a fish stick said.

I WOULDN'T EXIST WITHOUT MOLD!!

"Medics to the rescue!" Fry called out. He began tossing sodium benzoate powder in the air. It glittered in the bright lights of the Auditorium and slowly settled over everyone.

"It tingles!" a lumpy potato said.

When all the powder had been sprinkled, Slice, Fry, and Tootie began wrapping all the food in the Stay-Fresh-o-Lator. And before long, the grayish-green mold disappeared from every morsel in Belching Walrus Elementary. Even from Regimold.

"I'm me again!"

Regimold said. "It feels so nice. I feel so fresh!"

"Like a day at the spa!" a fuzzy peach said.

"Enough of this!" Spex said. "How many times will we be interrupted before we hear what the jury thinks?"

"But there is one important fact you haven't heard," Slice said. "It has to do with Tootie."

Everyone's eyes turned to the little tater tot.

Baron von Lineal cleared his throat. "What do you have to say, little one?" he asked.

Tootie stepped onto the stage. "It was *me* who went into the Library. It was me who left the ketchup footprints on the carpet."

A gasp spread through the Auditorium, followed by a whole lot of murmuring.

"I was trying to figure out a cure for the mold sickness," Tootie said. "In order to do that, I needed to do some research. I *had* to go into the Library to read about sodium benzoate. I also had to understand what it was like to be a mold zombie, so I wandered

around the school a bit. I walked like them. I made a mess like them. I groaned like them."

"It's singing," Regimold said.

Tootie giggled. "Okay, I sang like them," she said.

"So, it was *you* in the Library?" Spex said.

Tootie nodded. "I was trying to cure a serious sickness," she said.

The jury started to whisper to one another. Finally, Chip stood up.

"It is the decision of the jury that Totz is not guilty," he said.

Everyone cheered.

"But what about the other tater tot?" Spex said. "Arrest Tootie! Someone has to pay for the damage! Someone has to pay for breaking the rules!"

Baron von Lineal banged his gavel so hard that it broke into a thousand pieces.

"It is my decision that Tootie was acting in the best interest of the school. Belching Walrus Elementary is a better place because of what she did. She saved everyone in the

Cafeteria. Since there was no lasting damage, case dismissed."

Spex sank down in her seat and nodded. "I suppose you're right," she said. "Case dismissed."

A cheer, one even louder than before, spread through the Auditorium, and all the food took off their Stay-Fresh-o-Lator wrappings.

Totz ran over and gave Slice, Scoop, Fry, and Tootie huge hugs.

"I don't know how to thank you," Totz said.

"No need to thank us, buddy," Slice said. "You would have done the same for us."

"You would have done *more* for us," Scoop said. "After all, you can play the banjo, write wicked rhymes, and do cartwheels."

"Aw, that's nothing compared to winning your first case in court," Totz said. "You were amazing!"

"I guess there's only one thing left to do now," Slice said.

Everyone answered at once: "PARTY!"

**Missed what happened in the fourth Bad Food
adventure? Turn the page and find out!**

# CHAPTER 1
## Letting Off Steam

**A**s always, night had come to Belching Walrus Elementary. The doors were locked, the hallways were silent, and the intercom didn't let out a crackle. Oh, and everyone in the cafeteria was letting off steam.

No, what I meant to say is that every piece of food and every plate, fork, and spoon in the cafeteria at Belching Walrus Elementary come alive each night to have fun. Every night.

And ever since the folks from the other rooms in the school helped Slice, Scoop, and Totz stop the sneaky Class Pets from setting their traps . . .

Well, it's all been pretty good since then.

And, as always, best friends forever Slice (a brave

and cheesy slice of pizza), Scoop (a triple scoop ice cream cone—vanilla, chocolate, AND strawberry), and Totz (a crunchy, delicious, and trendy tater tot) were blowing off their own steam under the utility sink.

"Hey, where's Totz?" Slice said.

Scoop looked up from the painting she was working on. "I don't know," she said. "I've been too busy working on my newest creation."

She spun her canvas around. The painting was divided into four squares: one blue, one yellow, one green, and one pink. Each square had a painting of Scoop in it.

"It's a self-portrait," Scoop said.

Slice flexed his arms to make tiny muscles. "Wouldn't you rather paint a picture of me?"

Scoop laughed. "A self-portrait is more than just a picture," she said. "It shows how the artist sees themself."

Slice looked at the painting again. "So, you see yourself in four colored squares?"

Scoop rolled her eyes.

Just then, they heard a grunt. Totz was hanging upside down from a string above them.

"What are you doing?" Slice asked.

"Shhh . . . Act natural," Totz said. "I'm being a spy."

"How long have you been hanging up there?" Scoop asked.

"Too . . . long." Totz grunted.

Suddenly, the string let go and Totz fell.

He sprang to his feet and straightened his head-phones. "I told you to hold on to that string until I tugged three times," Totz called out, looking up.

Their egg friends, Sal and Monella, poked their faces over the edge of the sink.

"You're too heavy for our little hands," Sal said.

"Plus, we're late for our daily speed walk," Monella added.

And with that, Sal and Monella disappeared. Slice, Scoop, and Totz could hear them as they went off.

*Left, right, left, right, left, right . . .*

"Hey, nice self-portrait," Totz said. "It shows the many sides of you—similar but also different."

Scoop smiled and then glared at Slice. "At least someone gets me."

"So why do you want to be a spy?" Slice asked Totz.

"Now that I've learned to play the banjo, I need a new hobby," he explained. "I thought being a spy would be fun and interesting."

"What do you know about being a spy?" Slice asked.

"Plenty," Totz said, leaning against a box none of them had ever seen before. "We are always sneaking around and solving problems. Our friend Rasher can make gadgets. And I already have the sunglasses."

"Have you learned any spy skills?" Scoop said.
"Like what?" Totz asked.
"Like problem-solving," Slice said.

"Being a master of disguise," Scoop said.

"And blending in with other cultures," Slice said.

"Yup," Totz said. "I can do all those things."

Slice shrugged. "Then I guess you're on your way to being a spy."

Just then, a thump came from inside a cardboard box none of them had ever seen before.

A CARDBOARD BOX NONE OF THEM HAD EVER SEEN BEFORE

"Stand aside," a voice said. "Coming through."

It was Glizzy the hot dog. He came running over with Sprinkles the donut, who (as always) was trailing sprinkles behind her. Glizzy pressed his ear to the side of the box.

"Hello?!?" he called out. He knocked on the box and said it again. "Hello?!?"

Muffled voices came from inside.

Glizzy and Sprinkles placed their hands on the side of the box and pushed. It didn't budge.

"Slice, Scoop, Totz, can you please help us?" Sprinkles said.

The group rocked the box back and forth. Finally, it tipped over and the lid popped open.

Out marched dozens of donuts. Some were round with a hole in the middle, some were long and twisty, and some were stuffed on the inside. Some were glazed, some were frosted, some had sprinkles, and some had nothing at all. There were pink donuts, chocolate donuts, and a few that looked as though their sprinkles were baked right inside.

The largest of these donuts, a round fellow wearing an eyepatch, waddled out. He had short arms and legs and a perfect coating of purple frosting. Alongside him walked a much smaller, plain donut.